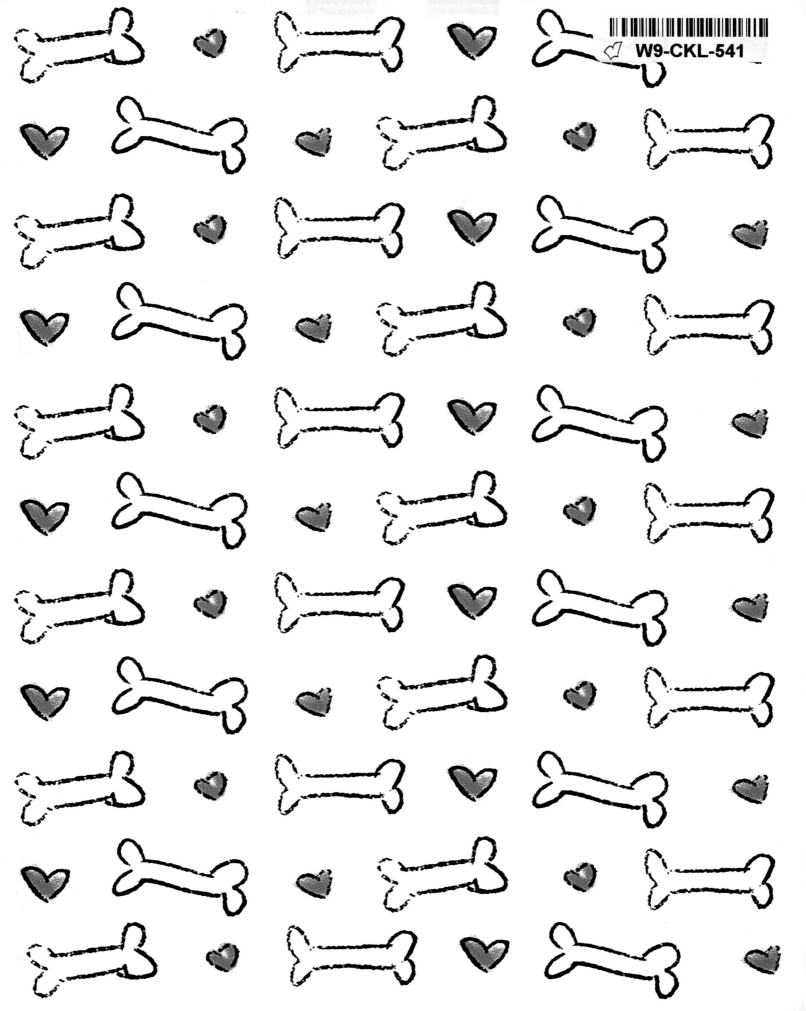

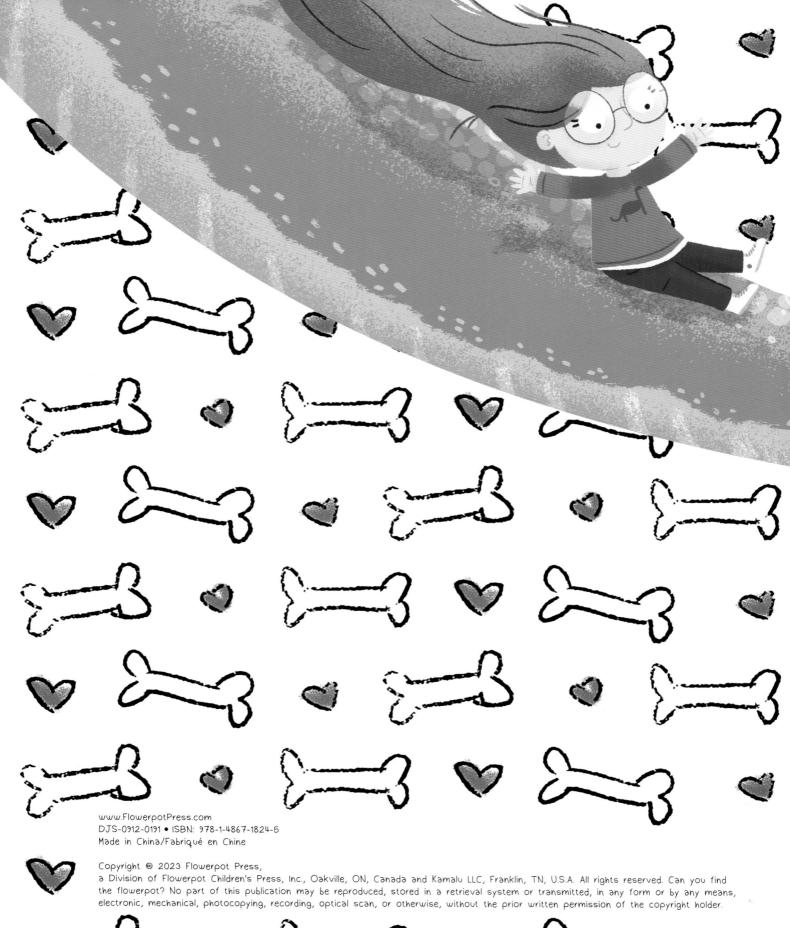

www.FlowerpotPress.com
DJS-0912-0191 • ISBN: 978-1-4867-1824-5
Made in China/Fabriqué en Chine

Dinos Are a Girl's Best Friend!

Written by Hayley Vaughters

Illustrated by Dean Gray

Dinos are a girl's best friend!

Stella's best friend is the
STEGOSAURUS.
(steh-guh-SORE-us)
She likes their pointy spikes.

Tyra's best friend is the
TYRANNOSAURUS REX.
(tai-ran-uh-SORE-us recks)
She likes how big and tall they are.

Trish's best friend is the
TRICERATOPS.
(try-SAIR-uh-tops)
She likes their cool horns.

Priya's best friend is the
PTERODACTYL.
(teh-ruh-DAK-tul)
She likes how they can fly.

Annie's best friend is the
ANKYLOSAURUS.
(an-ko-lo-SORE-us)
She likes their strong armor.

Paris's best friend is the
PACHYCEPHALOSAURUS.
(pack-ee-sef-uh-luh-SORE-us)
She likes their helmet-like head.

Megan's best friend is the
MEGALODON.
(MAY-guh-luh-dawn)
She likes their huge fins.

Theresa's best friend is the
THERIZINOSAURUS.
(thay-ruh-zeen-uh-SORE-us)
She likes their scissor-like claws.

Ariana's best friend is the
ARCHAEOPTERYX.
(ar-kee-OP-tuh-riks)
She likes their pretty feathers.

Veronica's best friend is the
VELOCIRAPTOR.
(vuh-LAH-suh-rap-ter)
She likes how fast they can run.

Brianna's best friend is the
BRACHIOSAURUS.
(brah-kee-uh-SORE-us)
She likes their long, curved necks.

Dinos are a girl's

best friend!

Tyrannosaurus rex was one of the largest dinosaurs of all time, growing over 40 feet long!

Triceratops had a beak like a parrot!

Archaeopteryx was very small, about the size of a pigeon.

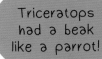

Pachycephalosaurus had such great eyesight that it was like they had binoculars for eyes!

Stegosaurus had a brain that was about the size of a hot dog.

Megalodon was twice as big as a great white shark!

Ankylosaurus had so much armor on its body that it even covered its eyelids.

Velociraptor was about the size of a turkey.

Pterodactyl had wings similar to a bird and a bat.

Brachiosaurus had a neck that was six times longer than a giraffe's!

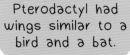

Therizinosaurus had the largest claws of any animal, even to this day!